THE NEW BIZARRO AUTHOR SERIES

PRESENTS

I0630134

AUNT POSTER
John Wayne Comunale

Eraserhead Press
Portland, OR

ERASERHEAD PRESS
P.O. BOX 10065
PORTLAND, OR 97296

WWW.ERASERHEADPRESS.COM

ISBN: 978-1-62105-234-0

Printed in the USA.

Acknowledgments

Thanks and love to Emily and Lindsay and BooTown always. Thanks to my doll Katy, and my bunny-beagle-pit Lebowski. Thank you to my MIcroSatan family, and Khod-man for the riffing of ideas. Most of all thank you to my Bizarro family, and the motivation you give me daily.

Foreword by Garrett Cook

John Wayne Comunale is a guy I know from BizarroCon. He's usually up really fucking late and is down for anything. He's a punk rocker and blows the roof off the place during the open mic parties. He's not what most people think when they think "writer." He's an extrovert, a performer and a big personality. And that's cool. John Wayne Comunale is fucking cool. He's fucking scary Texas punk rock cool.

John Wayne has created a coming-of-age novel like no coming-of-age novel you've ever seen before. The object of the young protagonist's affection is not just objectified but literally an object, a pinup poster on the wall of his uncle's garage. What seems like a running gag turns into a commentary on narcissism, feminism and coming-of-age novels themselves. It's funny, tense and sad. You hold in your hands a big idea presented in a fun, engaging way by a really cool guy. He's one of four authors handpicked this year to give you a glimpse of the genre's future and to introduce you, the reader, to new writers in the Bizarro community. If you like this, lend the author your support with a review, a post on social media or just by telling a friend. Enjoy the book!

Chapter One

There was a poster that hung in my uncle's house, but it was never in the same place for very long. The poster was well over twenty years old by the time I was introduced to her, but in much better condition than you would expect. It certainly wasn't what collectors would call 'mint,' but it was definitely not too shabby. The tears around the corners from years of thumbtacks being pushed in and haphazardly ripped out, along with the permanent crease marks that ran parallel to each other just left of center were more like beauty marks than flaws. They made the poster look refined. The blemishes gave her character. They were classic, deep-set features telegraphing a wisdom that came with age. They showed the poster had been cared for; she had been loved. This poster earned its marks from being taken down, and put back up more times than any poster probably should. More times than a poster like this, that's for sure.

It depicted a fairly attractive young woman. Pretty enough to be on a poster, at least. She had curly brown hair with subtle, non-threatening sun-kissed streaks that dappled her 'girl next door' look with the kind of soft-core sexiness that made you feel like you might have a chance. Simulated sunlight wrapped an amber glow around her dark auburn mane not unlike that of a saint's halo. The false heavenly light faded with airbrushed assistance into a sky too blue to be real. The woman on the poster was smiling but not showing her teeth, which always made me think she had something to hide.

She was wearing a red and black flannel shirt with the

sleeves cut off and the front tied up into a tight and tiny knot perched just below her ample breasts. This was obviously the characteristic she leaned on to make up for her less than stunning looks and secret smiles. The top two buttons of the torn and tied up shirt were unbuttoned to optimize her cleavage. She wore tattered, cutoff blue jean shorts with the appropriate amount of fray and fade to pay homage to the 'daisy duke' style. Her bare thighs and calves were tanned and shapely. They weren't quite as toned as you would expect from a girl on a poster.

On her feet were the kind of dark brown boots you see on people who work outside all day, but free of the dirt and scuffs that typically adorn this type of footwear. For her they served more of an aesthetic purpose than a practical one. Her hands were balled up into tiny fists that she planted firmly on her hips like she was punching herself in the midsection. Lying at her feet was the true star though. It was an automobile transmission shined and polished to a high gloss luster; a treatment that is traditionally never wasted on engine parts unless advertising is involved. The buxom woman rested her left foot on top of the transmission, while her right foot remained planted on a tuft of shiny plastic grass. Written across the bottom of the poster in a pointy, sharply angled font were yellow letters lined in black that said: *McKenzie Transmission.*

This was my Uncle's wife. Not the woman in the poster, but the poster itself. He married her back before I was born, so all I knew about what happened leading up to that momentous occasion is what my Dad would tell me. He loved his brother and the last thing he would ever want to do is paint him in a negative light, but not even he could mask his tone to hide the reservations he had with my Uncle's choices. He never said anything necessarily disparaging about my Uncle to me, but his true feelings showed through in his timbre and cadence. Even as a young man I could tell he didn't think this was the right woman for his brother

My Grandparents didn't exercise the same tact and discipline as my Dad. While my Grandmother would only go as far as to call him an 'odd duck' from time to time, it was my Grandfather who swung his opinion around like a battle-axe. He wouldn't hesitate to refer to his son as a 'damn dipshit weirdo,' 'touched in the head,' or even 'that crazy fucking asshole.' Luckily for my Uncle, they spent most of their time toiling away in their garden shed with a small candy making business they'd set up to stay busy since retiring. They called it *Power Candy*, but it smelled terrible and tasted worse, so they never had to worry about me eating up the profits.

My Uncle was mostly left alone, but even when Grandfather was at his most crotchety and foul-mouthed, my Uncle remained unaffected. I guess he was forced to develop a thick skin early in life in order to deflect his father's brutally harsh opinions of him.

I have no knowledge of the romantic endeavors my Uncle engaged in previous to Aunt Poster, but whenever I'd ask my Dad about it he would casually change the subject, never to bring the conversation back around to the original question. My guess was he was either uncomfortable talking about it, or didn't want to labor my young, developing brain with the task of making sense of my Uncle's love life. It didn't matter to me either way because I loved my Uncle very much. I also loved my Aunt Poster, but later came to develop feelings for her that I wasn't equipped to deal with. It turned out I understood my Uncle a little better than I realized, maybe even better than anyone else in the family, except for Aunt Poster of course. She understood us both far better than we could ever hope to understand ourselves.

Chapter Two

McKenzie Transmission had been a popular body shop back in the late seventies before I was born. They specialized in transmissions initially, but branched out into a full service shop that could do anything from oil changes to engine overhauls. They'd done so well, they eventually opened a second location across town that was managed by Mr. McKenzie's son, Junior. The second shop flourished even more than the first, prompting the McKenzie family to open a third shop, which they planned to do in a more central area of town. Unfortunately, their third location never got past the planning stages and the other two withered on the vine.

The true reason behind the McKenzie family's demise was supposedly mired in controversy and hearsay, but my Dad knew all about it. Apparently, Junior McKenzie let the minor amount of success he was experiencing go to his head, as often happens among the weak-minded nouveau-riche, and the spending of his sudden excess of disposable income got out of control. My Dad said Junior got himself and the family in trouble from circumstances brought about by the women he was 'courting,' who took advantage of him for his money.

To put it plainly, Junior McKenzie had a problem with the whores. He couldn't get enough of them, and he simply let his compulsion get out of control to the extent of sinking the business and financially ruining his family. It got to where he had more hookers come through his shop in a day than actual customers. He would take them into the pits. He finally turned one of pits into his private fuck-hole, which meant one less car could be serviced at a time. He didn't care about that though. He replaced all the motor oil, antifreeze, and wiper fluid with various lubricants, rubbers, and sex toys, the kind you had to send away for because they didn't sell those things in the town's only adult bookstore.

It wasn't all his fault though. Well, actually yes it was. It was totally his fault. Junior developed ultra-arrogance brought on by the inflated sense of importance and stature the success of his family's business gave him. His mind began to warp in a way that caused him to believe he held dominion over the prostitutes that visited him, and even though it was he who called for them to come, his faculties became so compromised by ego he believed it was the other way around. Because of this twisted thought process, he determined that he could pay his ladies of ill repute whatever he wanted based on how well he thought they performed, and not the rates that were communicated to him upfront.

While it wasn't uncommon for him to pay a hundred bucks for a twenty-dollar blowjob when he thought they really deserved it, his generous moments were few and far between. The norm for Junior became low-balling hookers for what he deemed sub-par performance. As you can imagine, this didn't go on for long once word got back to the pimps that some grease monkey was stiffing their bitches. One night, Junior was met at his home by said pimps who proceeded to exercise the strength of their pimp hands all over him. The next morning, Junior was found dead and naked, splayed out face down on his front yard. The pimps had beaten him to death, ransacked his house, and took everything of value with them. One of them pulled the American flag from his porch on their way out, and jammed the splintered pole it was waving from right up Junior's ass, making for a gruesomely patriotic picture. On the way out of town, they stopped at Junior's shop, burned it to the ground, and left a letter for old man McKenzie saying they wanted the money Junior owed them or he was next.

When Mr. McKenzie found out his son was dead, and that he was now responsible for his tremendous debt, he dropped dead of a heart attack. Not even his sizeable life insurance policy could bail the family out. They were forced to close the one shop that was left and sell everything in it. This included tools, machinery, equipment, waiting room chairs, and of course all advertising materials, including posters.

Chapter Three

Around the time McKenzie's was closing, my Dad and Uncle were putting together plans to build a hotrod. They had the frame, but that was about it, and they thought they'd be able to find everything else they would need in the salvage yard or the dump. When they heard McKenzie's was selling everything, they figured it would be a great opportunity to pick up some parts and tools for dirt cheap, which was great because they were both pretty broke.

I knew this story pretty well, because my Dad told it to me more than a few times, and never while sober.

"You know where we met your Aunt?" My Dad would slur when he was half way into a bottle of Beam.

Don't get me wrong here, I don't want to paint the picture of my Dad being some drunkard who told me crazy shit each time he hit the sauce. My Dad actually didn't drink that often, but when he did, it was in large quantities. And he only drank when he was in the garage working on one of his many projects. My Dad had the attention span of a gnat, so large swaths of time would pass between his visits to the garage, and even then, he would usually start an entirely new project.

He would look at a pile of disjointed, half built mystery pieces and struggle to remember what they could have been. That was when he would pull a bottle down from the cabinet over his workbench, one of the few projects he saw through to the end, and slide the mess onto the floor, abandoning the lost idea for the next soon to be doomed project. I watched my Dad begin and never finish a bookshelf for my room

13

eleven different times. My books are in a pile by the toilet to this very day.

Despite this constant self-imposed setback to all of Dad's projects, I still loved the time I spent with him in the garage listening to him slur his way through the same few stories over and over again, sometimes pissing himself and passing out in the process. According to him, he doesn't remember any of the time we spent in the garage together, but if he could, I bet he would feel the same way about it as I do.

My Dad told me the story of how my Uncle met Aunt Poster many times, but my favorite was the first time. Maybe it was the newness of the story, or maybe it was what sparked the slurry of emotions I would soon come to experience. It might have been neither of those things, but for some reason he never told the story with the same fervor as that first time. Maybe the event resonated with him less and less as he got older, or maybe this is just the way I've chosen to remember it. Either way, it went like this:

"You know where he met your Aunt? It was down at McKenzie's while they were going out of business. They were having one of those *everything must go and go now* type of sales, so your Uncle and I thought we'd go down and see if we could find any parts for the . . . hotrod we were supposed to build that summer."

My Dad also told me the story of said hotrod several times as well, and it was clearly a sore spot many years later. I'll spare you the details, but needless to say, the hotrod never got built, and, for reasons I've never fully understood, it has something to do with Faye Dunaway, whose name and the names of any of her movies we are never allowed to say. Never. But, that's not relevant to this story.

"We split up when we got there, and I started picking through bins looking for anything useful. I found a couple wrenches that weren't completely beat to shit, and a bag of sparkplugs that looked gently used, but aside from that it was all junk. Everything useful was pretty well picked over already.

"When I went looking for your Uncle, I couldn't find him anywhere. I paid for the wrenches and sparkplugs, and went to check outside. I could see from across the parking lot that he was sittin' in the passenger seat of the car staring down into his lap. Not the regular kind of 'off into space' type staring either. This was some real hardcore, mesmerized type staring. It was kinda' creepy.

"I told him the whole place had been picked clean when I got in the car, then asked if there was anything we could use.

He didn't say anything. He didn't even look up. It was like he was under a spell or something.

"After a few more seconds of silence he answered, but he didn't look up when he did. He just said, 'Poster.'

Then, he repeated it. 'Poster.'

I finally followed his gaze down to his lap, and saw the poster he was talking about.I said, "You got one of their old transmission posters. I'm pretty sure that girl went to high school with us. What was her name? Terry? Claire? Blaire? I can't remember, but I do know her tits were definitely not that big back then. She must have a great doctor. I wonder if she still . . ."

He cut me off. He said, "Hey! Don't talk about her like that!"

His tone had changed, but his eyes never left the poster.

I asked if he kn"ew her, if he was carrying a torch for someone, but he didn't say anything back, so I just started driving home. We drove along in silence for most of the way until your Uncle just blurted it out."He said, 'I love her,' and I thought he meant the girl on the poster. I asked if he kept in touch with her. Hadn't she moved away years ago? And what was her name again?

Vicki? Jenny? Jasmine?

"Not the girl!" he said. "I don't know who she is, or if she went to school with us. I'm talking about the poster. I love this poster."

"I couldn't figure out what the hell he was talking about." He just kept repeating, "I'm in love with this poster."

That was all he said for the rest of the drive. When we got home, he went right to his room for the rest of the night. And he never stopped staring at Aunt Poster either. He didn't come out to help with the hotrod and he didn't come out for dinner or to watch his favorite show, *Manimal*. It was the *Scrimshaw* episode too, and he never missed that one!

"Anyway, I didn't think much of it and just let him be for the night. I figured in the morning he'd have abandoned his whole 'poster love' notion, and be ready to start on the hotrod, but oh no, not your Uncle. When he didn't come down for breakfast I decided to go pull him out of bed. He wasn't in his room though, and his drawers were hanging limp and empty from the dresser. His window was open, and a note was taped to the sill that said he'd run off to start a new life with his true love, the poster. It went on to say he knew we wouldn't understand but he couldn't fight destiny. "

Your Grandmother she cried for a day or so before getting over it and eventually falling back into her routine of working on garden shed projects. Your Grandfather, on the other hand, wasn't as sympathetic, and only had one thing to say.

"Your brother is a weird little fucker."

And yeah, I knew it, but we all did.

Chapter Four

That was the last the family saw of my Uncle for the rest of the summer. After the first week, everyone stopped worrying about him, and after two weeks, everyone was so used to him being gone they forgot what it was like to have him around. It was easy for them to forget about him, because forgetting about a member of your family being in love with a poster is easier if you don't have to deal with it on a daily basis.

Over the course of the next three months, several odd postcards were delivered to the house depicting unknown roadside stops from all across the country. I say roadside stops and not attractions because there was certainly nothing attractive about the places these things came from. The first one to arrive depicted a landscape the pallid hue of a withered and bloodless ghoul tossed aside by a satiated vampire. A bright blue, cloudless sky struck a thick line of contrast against the bleak landscape. The ground in the picture actually was as desolate and depressing as it appeared, and didn't need to rely on trick photography to illustrate the point.

Day-glow pink and yellow words were scribbled whimsically across the bottom of the photo that said:

Welcome to Burnt Stump, Iowa.
Wish we WEREN'T here! LOL!

No message was written on the back, but telltale greasy fingerprints smeared across the photo let everyone know the correspondence was without a doubt from my Uncle. Other postcards arrived from places like *Butt-Wart, Montana*;

Shaft-Hair, Arkansas; *Ingrown, Indiana;* and *Gangrenous, Georgia*. These postcards still exist, kept in an old cigar box on my Uncle's bookshelf to this day.

The summer was finally loosening its fiery stranglehold, with fall slipping through the cracks, and there hadn't been a postcard in over two weeks. The family thought they truly had heard the last of my Uncle, until he burst through the backdoor during supper on the last day of August.

He was wearing a tuxedo t-shirt with the sleeves cut off, and the only pair of jeans he owned. His belt was unbuckled, and dangled at either side of his crotch framing it in tarnished brass, and frayed leather. In his right hand he held the poster just as he had the last time the family had seen him, and in his right was a mostly empty bottle of champagne.

"Good news, everyone," he slurred stumbling into the table and upsetting the casserole dish. "I'm home and I'm married! Say hello to my bride."

He held up the poster for the family to congratulate while he stared lovingly into her eyes.

My Dad waited to take his cue to speak from Grandfather, who just shrugged and kept shoving tuna-noodles into his face.

"Well, you know I've always wanted grandchildren," my grandmother said. "Now buckle your pants and sit down if you want me to make you a plate."

And just like that, my Uncle slipped right back into the family, never missing an opportunity to ingratiate his new bride to them. Like most couples at the beginning of a relationship, they were inseparable, and wherever my Uncle happened to be in the house, Aunt Poster would be hanging on a wall close by. She hung in the living room when he watched television, over her designated place at the dinner table, and even in the bathroom over the toilet while my Uncle showered. The bathroom was her favorite spot in the house, as I would later come to find.

When my Uncle went to run errands or hang out with friends, he would simply pluck Aunt Poster from the wall, roll her up, set her in the passenger seat of his car, and bring her along. My Dad said he would see Aunt Poster 'hanging' out with my Uncle at the local bar, Chubby's, where she would watch him drunkenly play pool, or throw darts with his friends from a wall next to the bathroom. My Aunt was never really a 'bar person,' but she would go because she knew it made my Uncle happy. She was just really supportive like that. She was a pleaser.

Uncle tried to spend every waking moment with her as if it physically pained him to be away. It might not have been so awkward for everyone if my Uncle actually had a job, and was out of the house for a portion of the day, but he hadn't been employed since long before he'd run off with Aunt Poster. My Grandmother would nudge my Uncle to start looking for a job, reminding him he had a wife to take care of now, and he couldn't rely on his 'good looks' to get by in life.

My Grandfather, on the other hand, was not subtle or gentle in what he had to say on the matter. Particularly when he found Aunt Poster hanging on the wall inside the garden shed where he and my Grandmother made their Power Candy. He ripped her down turning two of her corners into uneven, lopsided tears that frayed at the ends, and stormed into the house waving around Aunt Poster while screaming at my Uncle.

"You weird little fucker! You and your wife stay the hell out of my shed! Neither of you have any business snooping around in there. And another thing, by this time next week I want your poster-loving ass to be employed, or both of you are out on the streets!"

With that he threw Aunt Poster across the room where

she hit the wall, and slid down between the piano and end table. My Dad said this was how her creases started, but my Uncle would never talk about the incident. He was furious because he hadn't been in the garden shed with Aunt Poster, and had no idea why she'd go somewhere without him. My Uncle carefully pulled Aunt Poster out from behind the piano, rolled her up slowly and gingerly, and took her up to his room without saying a word. My Dad said he went up to check on him shortly after, but decided to leave him alone when he heard him sobbing from down the hall.

My Dad felt bad for his brother, and knew their parents were pressuring him because he himself had gotten a decent job, and was about to move into an apartment with my Mom. He decided he'd help his brother get a job before he officially moved out of the house.

The next morning, when my Dad came down to breakfast, he found my Uncle at the table by himself wearing the only suit he owned. It was an ill-fitting, pale blue monstrosity he'd gotten from Sears almost five years ago, and only wore once in an attempt to make himself appear older so a store clerk would sell him beer. Needless to say, it didn't work, and my Uncle chucked the suit in a corner. Judging by the shape it was in, it had more than likely stayed in that corner until this morning.

Uncle was drinking coffee and eating breakfast while perusing the comic section of the paper. Aunt Poster was not hanging in her normal breakfast spot. She was nowhere to be seen.

My Uncle told my Dad he'd lined up two interviews for that morning, and was spending the rest of the afternoon pounding the pavement to look for any other opportunities he could find. He said he let Aunt Poster sleep in since she'd stayed up almost all night helping him look for jobs and coaching him on what to say in his interviews. He asked that my Dad take care in being quiet while walking down the hallway upstairs since she was such a light sleeper and really needed to catch up on her rest. With that, he was out the door and on his way to finding a job. Since my Dad didn't have to help him he decided to spend the day with my Mom getting things prepared for their impending move.

Chapter Five

It turns out when you make Power Candy in your garden shed there's a very high probability of blowing yourself all the way the hell up, which is unfortunately what happened while the two brothers were out seizing the day. My Dad said that when he turned on the street to come home, a barrier of fire trucks, ambulances, and police cars kept him from getting anywhere near the house. He saw my Uncle's car parked halfway up into the neighbor's yard with the driver side door open and the engine still running.

My Dad pulled his car to the curb three houses away seeing the pillar of thick black smoke rising from the backyard of his family's home. He leapt from his car and ran toward the house, but was stopped by a police officer who let him through only after he emphatically screamed that he lived there. He ran around to the backyard where several firefighters were trying their best to extinguish a white-hot fireball that had once been the garden shed. The chief yelled orders to his hose-wielding subordinates as they battled a blaze that seemed to only gain intensity when doused by the high-pressure water stream.

The fire chief waved my Dad off shouting something unintelligible at him as he bolted past the firemen, and through the back door of the house. He called to my Grandparents because at the time he had no idea they'd been vaporized in the garden shed when it exploded. He went from room to room calling and searching until he found my Uncle in his bed crying and clutching Aunt Poster.

"She's okay," sobbed my Uncle tightly grasping at the

sides of Aunt Poster while being careful not to lie directly on top of her. "I was so worried when I pulled up, but I found her safe and sound in bed."

"What about Mom and Dad?" asked my Dad shakily. "Where are they? Are they okay?"

My Uncle ignored him turning his attention to Aunt Poster comforting her with reassuring kisses.

"It's okay my darling," he said to her between soft smooches, "it's okay. Everything will be okay."

My Dad tried to pull his brother from the bed to snap him out of it and make him answer, but it was no use. My Uncle held tight to the headboard, refusing to move or break eye contact with Aunt Poster. Dad left him there to go search the rest of the house, but as he exited the room, he swore he caught a glimpse of a blackened singe mark on the bottom left corner of Aunt Poster. It didn't register with him at the time, but hours later, when everything was over and he knew his parents were in fact very dead, he remembered what he saw.

My Uncle was in the kitchen staring off into space with a cup of coffee in front of him that had long since gone cold. Aunt Poster was hanging in her usual kitchen-spot between the telephone and the spice rack. My Dad was pretending to be on the phone, but was really examining the corners of Aunt Poster. Three of them bore familiar tatters and tears, but the bottom left had been clearly cut, leaving a perfectly straight line that erased any signs of use or age

"Whatcha' looking at?" said my Uncle.

Dad didn't answer. Instead, he picked up the phone to call his bride to be and tell her the news.

Chapter Six

My Dad didn't stay at the house that night, or any other night after that. Ever. He stayed with my Mom at her parents house until their apartment was ready to move into. There were no remains of Grandma and Grandpa left that the fire department could find, citing the ultra-intense heat as the culprit. There wasn't even really any mess to clean up after the fire was out either. A charred black square was the only evidence it ever existed. After the memorial service, my Dad moved the rest of his things out of the house and left it to his brother and his wife to have. It was for the best since my Uncle's behavior had gotten so erratic that he was just plain hard to be around. My Dad said he just couldn't trust Aunt Poster.

My Dad figured the house would be in complete and utter disrepair within a matter of weeks. He couldn't have been more wrong. On the day my Grandparents were quite literally blown off the planet, my Uncle's tenacity driven initiative paid off. He was hired on as the lead activator down at the old activation plant on the edge of town. He couldn't actually be a lead activator until he passed his training and put in his time. Until then, he would remain at temporary co-activator status.

My Dad lost contact with his brother for a while after the accident, but he would often drive past the old house, expecting to see it crumbling to he ground, on fire, or completely gone from an explosion similar to the one that turned the garden shed into ash. But the house was always in great shape. The lawn was always mowed and manicured.

Grandfather had never kept the yard looking that good. He thought caring too much about your lawn was a sign of weakness, and he was a man who could not abide the appearance of weakness. The more Dad drove by the house, the more improvements he saw done to it. There was a fresh coat of paint on the exterior. The banister around the front porch had been rebuilt and included ornate, hand carved filigree across the well-sanded wood.

One day, he drove by and actually saw his brother outside planting rose bushes up against the house. He decided he needed to stop and pull over. He got out and walked up to where his brother was carefully digging a perfect hole in the soft soil he'd filled the beds with earlier in the day.

"What are you doing?" my Dad asked him.

"I'm planting rose bushes," answered my Uncle matter-of-factly. "It's good to see you by the way. It's been a—"

"Yeah, I can see you're planting rose bushes, but that's not what I mean. What I mean is what are you doing with the house? The paint, the lawn, the porch, and now this? The place looks great! What gives man?"

"You like it? I've just been steadily working on small projects here and there since mom and dad passed. I wanted to make the house a little more comfortable for the little lady and me, so I decided to change some things. Let me show you what I've done inside."

He tossed his spade into the soft soil and the tilled dirt swallowed it down to the wooden handle. My Dad followed him up the porch steps and into the house, not sure what to expect. If what was happening on the outside of the house was any indication, than the inside should be incredible. On the other hand, my Dad knew his brother well, or at least thought he did, so there was a strong possibility that he would be walking into a broken down trash pit that would send even the most dedicated of hoarders into mental collapse.

"So, as you can see," said my Uncle upon ushering my Dad through the front door, "the missus and I have been pretty busy fixing up the old place. It's still a work in progress, but we're getting there."

Calling what they'd done to the childhood home my Dad hadn't set foot in since his parents died a 'work in progress' was an egregious understatement. Just what my Dad could see from the entryway made him feel like he was in a different house altogether. The faded yellow walls of the short hall that led to the living room had been painted a bright and vibrant shade of lilac. The old family photos that had lined the hall his entire life were gone, replaced by updated pictures of Aunt Poster with my Uncle at various places around the country. My Dad guessed they were taken during the summer the two were traveling because he recognized the backgrounds from some of the postcards the family had received over those three months.

"We've updated the living room a bit," said my Uncle.

This statement was also grossly inaccurate. The cracked and peeling paint that matched the hall had been scraped away and painted over with a deep red that contrasted nicely with the lilac. Their father's ratty old recliner had been replaced by one of those new, state-of-the-art, leather models with a cooler built into the side and cup holders in each arm. The 1970's era, pea-green Davenport had been traded out as well for a leather sofa that matched the recliner. There was an oversized wedding portrait of Aunt Poster and my Uncle that was clearly taken at a Las Vegas drive-thru wedding chapel. I myself have studied that portrait many times, finding it hard to believe how absolutely stunning Aunt Poster looks in it, but I guess all women look stunning in their wedding photos. My Uncle is smiling a smile I've never seen on his face in real life, and while my Dad tells me the expression is 'chemically induced,' I don't believe him. I think the smile is genuine, and can honestly say I have never seen such happiness between two people captured on film in my entire short life.

My Uncle took my Dad through to the dining room, which was the most radically different room in the house he'd seen so far. No longer was it to serve the purpose of partaking in family meals as it now bore a distinct air of health and fitness. The carpet was gone, and replaced by hardwood planks with colorful rubber mats splayed across it. The far wall along which the china hutch had resided was now covered from floor to ceiling in mirrors. There were also various workout accessories, such as medicine balls, and some kind of elastic rope pulley system.

"Oh, hey, honey," my Uncle said, addressing the far wall. "I didn't mean to bother you, but look who stopped by! I was just showing him some of the things we've been working on."

My Dad didn't even notice Aunt Poster hanging on the wall across the room until my Uncle spoke to her.

"This is just the beginning, right, sugar plum?" My Uncle went over to Aunt Poster and gave her a light peck on the cheek. "I know, I know you're all sweaty but I don't mind. You know, she plans on opening her own yoga studio someday, but this will have to do for now."

"Oh, really?" My Dad asked, still trying to take in the drastic changes his brother had made to the house.

"Yes sir," my Uncle replied emphatically. "She really is one of the best I've ever seen, and she's only getting better. Three or four of the ladies in the neighborhood come by a few times a week for classes now, but the word is spreading."

"That's . . . that's great," my Dad stammered. "Congratulations."

Over the next half hour my Uncle showed my Dad around the rest of the house, which was now completely foreign to him. My Uncle told him about future plans they had and about how well his job was going. Apparently, the activation market was booming, and my Uncle was poised on the forefront. He'd moved up faster than anyone else at the plant and was on his way to becoming head lead activator. My Dad was overcome with how impressed he was with the change in his brother. He'd gone from being an aimless, lazy fuck-up to a purpose-driven go-getter. Despite his reservations about Aunt Poster, it seemed that her influence on my Uncle's life was the best thing that could have happened to him. Maybe he'd been mistaken in his earlier suspicions?

The two brothers spent the rest of the afternoon reconnecting, and catching each other up on what had been happening in their lives. This was when my Dad broke the news to my Uncle that he was going to be an Uncle, because my Mom had just found out she was pregnant with me. The news of my impending entrance into the world was enough cause for the two to bury the hatchet and get over any bad blood that had occurred between them. Soon, they were spending weekends together, having dinner every Sunday, and my Dad would even stop by after work to help with whatever current home improvement project his brother was working on at the time. My Mom and Dad fully embraced Aunt Poster into the family, and my Mom even took some yoga classes from her specifically for pregnant women. Everything was going great, and it looked like Aunt Poster was here to stay. Then, I came along . . .

Chapter Seven

The years went by and the family unit of my Mom, Dad, Uncle, and Aunt Poster only grew stronger with the addition of me. We celebrated my first five birthdays in the house my Uncle had worked so hard to make his own. Despite the aesthetic differences, the house still had a strong and familiar sense of family running through it, which served to make it such an important place in my life. A place I would experience things that would help shape my life's path, and leave an indelible impression on me.

My parents were eventually able to save enough money to buy a house in the same old neighborhood just a few blocks away from my Aunt and Uncle's. I was in middle school and enjoyed splitting my time between both houses. I would hang out with my Uncle some days after school before my parents got home if I didn't feel like being alone at our house, which was often. Aunt Poster was usually busy teaching yoga, but my Uncle was always off from the plant by three so it worked out perfectly. We would mostly play catch in the backyard, or I'd help him with the rose bushes. If it were raining out, he'd let me sit in the recliner and watch all the monster movies my parents wouldn't let me watch.

Sometimes Aunt Poster would hang in the living room with me while I watched, but she was mostly going over curriculum for her classes. I also figured she was in there to make sure I didn't watch anything too crazy and violent for my young mind to process. I'd been around my Aunt Poster my whole life, so I was used to never seeing her hung in the same place for very long, but one day I found her hanging somewhere I'd personally never seen her hang before. It was on one of the rainy days and I was at their house after school watching *Return of the Kiss of Dracula's Kiss*, which I had been particularly excited to see. I drank almost four *Super Sugar Soda Bomb* sodas and was holding in my piss until I couldn't take it. I paused the movie and raced to the bathroom. I pushed through the door hard enough to cause it to bounce off the wall and almost smack me in the face. I threw open the toilet, and started yanking at my pants so I could let my soda dam burst into my porcelain salvation, but before I could get my wang past my zipper, I glanced up to see Aunt Poster hanging above the toilet.

"Oh shit! I mean, shoot," I said, jumping back trying, to pull my zipper up. "I'm sorry Aunt Poster, I didn't know you were in here."

Embarrassed beyond belief, I darted from the bathroom, shut the door behind me, and patiently waited outside for her to finish. The minutes ticked by at an excruciatingly slow pace due to the explosive pressure building in my loins. I decided to knock to let her know of my impending emergency.

"Aunt Poster, I'm sorry about barging in again. I just wanted to see if you were almost done. I gotta go real bad is all."

No answer. I knocked lightly again, but she didn't respond. About that time my Uncle had woken from the nap he was taking in their bedroom, and came down the hall.

"What's up, sport?" he asked, wiping the sleep from his eyes.

"Oh, nothing," I said looking at the carpet. "I have to pee really bad, but I'm waiting for Aunt Poster to come out."

"Well, you might be waiting for a while," he said.

I answered with a confused look, afraid that if I talked I would lose the small bit of control I still had over my bladder.

"That's her new meditation spot," he continued. "There's something about it being the only place in the house that allows her energy to align her chakras correctly. I don't understand all that stuff, but if it makes her happy, it's alright with me."

"So, what do I do?"

"Just go ahead in there and go. She won't mind. She's probably so deep in meditation she won't even know you're there."

"I don't think I can do that . . ."

"Well, you can't sit out here and piss yourself, now can you?"

My Uncle pushed open the door, and gave me a light push through.

"Just go ahead and go," he said closing the door behind me. "No telling how long she might be in there."

I stood in the bathroom frozen afraid to look up at my Aunt Poster, but the urge to relieve myself was quickly overcoming any impending and potential embarrassment. I stood in front of the toilet again, unzipped my zipper, but didn't expose myself right away.

"Aunt Poster?" I said still without looking up at her. "Can you hear me?"

There was still no answer, and I slowly looked up to see that she was most certainly locked into a deep meditative state. I quickly yanked out my unit and allowed my urine to finally escape to its final destination. It was the longest piss I can remember taking to this day, and I squeezed my eyes shut with satisfaction as I voided my bladder. I finally finished, shook out the last few drops, and tucked my modest manhood back into my pants. I leaned over to flush the toilet, and my eyes inadvertently wandered up to meet Aunt Poster's. They were no longer closed in meditation. She had been watching me.

31

Chapter Eight

That wasn't the first time Aunt Poster had been in the bathroom at the same time as me. My Uncle was right about that being her favorite place to meditate, and since it was usually just she and my Uncle in the house, it didn't seem like such a big deal. My own parents often shared the bathroom, one showering while the other was dressing or engaged in some other form of grooming, so it seemed to me like this was a norm among married people. I was one of the few people who was ever in the house with my Aunt and Uncle, so it was almost like I was intruding on their daily routines and rituals anyway. They didn't need to change the way they did things just because I was there for a few hours, and besides, we were family. We're supposed to be okay with each other's idiosyncrasies.

These are the things I told myself every time I slowly opened the bathroom door to find Aunt Poster perched above the porcelain throne like an ancient gargoyle guarding the entrance of a sacred chapel. Despite my rationalization, it still took me a while to get used to her occupying the bathroom at the same time as me.

At first I would avoid looking up at her as I stood at the mouth of the toilet, doing my best to distract myself from succumbing to urinary anxiety. I would just push it out as fast as I could, flush, and hurry off without as much as looking at or saying a word to Aunt Poster. I would repeat the same routine if I had to go number two as well, doing my best to evacuate my bowels in record speed while I felt her eyes burning into the back of my head.

This routine of avoidance went on for months until I just got used to it. I didn't say comfortable with it, just used to it. We never talked about the awkwardness of the situation either, but that was probably because it was only awkward for me. Everything was totally normal when Aunt Poster and I watched monster movies, or when we all sat down for dinner together, but I still felt a tension between us that would eventually need to be addressed in order for me to achieve the comfortability I so desperately desired. Little did I know that comfortability would come exactly one week into my freshman year. I was a late bloomer despite being a year older than my classmates on account of me having a birthday on the cusp of the class cutoff. Having a year up on everyone still wasn't enough to prepare me for the whirlwind of hormones dispatched to my system upon starting high school.

All of a sudden I was going to school with women instead of girls, and I found myself wanting to be near these women. Talk to these women. Smell these women. My body was sending my brain sexual signals that it didn't know how to interpret, so I would go into full-on meltdown mode if I even thought about talking to a girl, let alone smelling one. I was wading out into murky waters I had no idea how to navigate, and even though it got deeper with each step, I couldn't stop walking.

Luckily, I'd discovered masturbation, and just in the nick of time too because backed up semen was starting to push its way out of my tear ducts. If I'm to understand from a few of my male friends in whom I confided such things, there's apparently a feeling of shame that often accompanies masturbation. I, on the other hand, not only felt no shame or remorse for doing it, I felt like I'd let myself down if I didn't masturbate as many times as possible. I looked at it as if I was ejaculating poison from my body, which, if left unchecked, would paralyze my mind and cripple my body.

Not only did I not feel bad about the act of masturbating itself, I also didn't feel bad about how often I did it. It was as casual an act for me as checking my watch. Jerking off was honestly the only way to center myself and come back to a baseline so I could go on with my day. Once I felt the urge, if I didn't take care of it right away, I would became frazzled, and my focus would wane by the second. I wondered if this was how drug addicts felt during their pre-fix woes when all their mental and physical faculties aligned with the sole task of getting high. If a drug addiction was anything like this, I don't think I would have the willpower to ever get clean.

On one particular day, towards the beginning of my self-imposed masturbation endurance training, I was walking to my Uncle's house after school and found myself with a bit of a problem on my hands. From out of nowhere, I'd been struck by a surprise boner that possessed the combined strength of ten regular boners. It wasn't like this was the first time something like this had happened to me, but surprise boners were usually inadvertently triggered by something I thought about or saw. It wouldn't need to necessarily be something sexual to affect me this way, but at least my boner had a traceable origin. This one, on the other hand, did not, and judging by the way it was doing its damnedest to rip through the tight-knit denim of my jeans, I knew it wasn't happy about appearing unprovoked.

I was still two and half blocks from my Uncle's house, and although I told myself I wasn't ready to beat off in public yet, I was very close to lifting my moratorium on that belief. I tried to move as fast as the angry erection would let me, but with every step, the friction of the boner against my jeans sent mixed signals of pain and pleasure to my brain, further clouding my judgment. Soon, I was contemplating standing behind Mrs. Roddenberry's bushes or old man Fink's trashcans, but luckily I was able to exert enough willpower to keep it in my pants for the rest of the hurried walk.

My Uncle's front door was like an oasis in the desert, and not a moment too soon either. I burst through the front door, threw my backpack against the wall, called out a quick 'hey, it's me' to whoever could have been in earshot, and sprinted to the bathroom.

I shut the door, having the presence of mind to lock it, and released my confused cock from the constrictive confines of my pants. My dick throbbed in sync with my heartbeat as I took it in my hand, and held tight for fear that it might rocket off. I didn't waste time looking for lotion or tissues. I just started beating away with the reckless abandon of a boy who had nothing to lose.

I was jerking my dick like I was trying to beat the land speed record, and I was very quickly approaching climax. Maybe I'd had my eyes shut, or maybe I just had tunnel vision, but for whatever reason, in the moment before I was about to ejaculate I looked up in the mirror to see Aunt Poster hanging in her usual spot over the toilet behind me. If she had been meditating she wasn't anymore, but she hadn't said anything to get my attention. She was just . . . watching.

As weird as I think I should have felt about this, I had no negative emotions about Aunt Poster watching me masturbate. I actually liked it. I liked it so much that, as soon as we made eye contact, the swollen tip of my surprise boner exploded with a record setting amount of semen, covering the mirror with a jizz spray so fantastic some might say it had an artistic quality. Other people might say, 'Dang, that's a lot of cum!'

By the time my crisis was alleviated, and I'd fully and thoroughly rid myself of the 'poison,' the mirror was so thoroughly coated in ejaculate I couldn't see Aunt Poster's reflection anymore. I slowly removed my hand from my wilting member, slapped it against the mirror, and wiped a swath of the sticky mess away. Through the cloudy, translucent streaks there was one tiny clear spot big enough for me to see her eyes. They weren't angry, or judgmental, or embarrassed, but instead, held a warm kindness within them. Aunt Poster's eyes were telling me that not only what I'd just done was okay, but that I was okay too. They were telling me I didn't have anything to worry about, and in that moment, at least, I didn't.

Suddenly, there was a banging on the bathroom door strong enough to shake it on its hinges, and I became startlingly aware of the huge, sticky mess I'd made of the bathroom.

"You almost done in there?" called my Uncle from the other side of the door. "I've got a pretty severe emergency on deck here, so if you can just pinch it off and finish up in the yard or something, that'd be ideal."

I broke eye contact with Aunt Poster, devastated that this moment had to end so abruptly, and out of either of our control.

"Just a sec," I hollered at the door. "Let me . . . wipe first."

I looked around for something I could sop up the quickly drying jizz I'd deposited around the bathroom, and landed on the hand towel that hung next to the sink. It was pea soup green, and as far as I knew, had never been changed out because it was the only towel I'd ever seen hung there. I suppose it was possible that my Aunt and Uncle had several of these towels and would cycle them out every few days, but I doubted it. The purpose of this towel was for you to dry your hands after using the bathroom, but I don't think I'd used it in all the years I'd been aware of its existence. If I even washed my hands after using the bathroom, which was rare, I'm pretty sure I just dried them on my jeans, or just shook them until they were dry enough for me to not care anymore.

I snatched the towel from the hook by the mirror, and could tell by the texture it had not been washed in some time. The threads were coarse and stiff making for a jarring and unpleasant tactile experience. The thing already felt like it had been used to clean more than a few semen related messes, and I prayed it had one more left in it. I tried to wipe the mirror, but by this time, the fluid had firmed up considerably into semi-gelatinous blobs that stuck to the glass. The patches that weren't already completely dry were still just moist enough to leave a slime-streak trail in the towel's wake much like I'd seen snails leave across the leaves of my Uncle's rose bushes. I applied more pressure to my wiping, succeeding in only making a bigger mess.

"I really need to get in there," my Uncle called through the door, knocking urgently once again. "You don't even need to flush or anything, just let me in!"

The doorknob rattled furiously, and I thought for sure the lock was going to break any second. I stopped wiping, stepped back from the mirror, and turned around to face Aunt Poster. The expression on my face communicated the absolute desperation I felt far better than words ever could. Her eyes told me through their delicate expressiveness that I had nothing to worry about, and I could think of no reason to not trust them. With only a glance, Aunt Poster let me know that she would take care of everything, and I knew she would. The churning ocean of panic in my gut subsided, and the tension in my muscles melted away, loose and relaxed.

I balled up the filthy towel, threw it in the sink, and opened the bathroom door. I was thrown of balance as my Uncle burst through, but I caught myself on the towel rack.

"Sorry, boy, but my ass is approaching defcon-5. I got no time to lose!"

I hurried out through the door and closed it behind me. The primal sounds of my Uncle's bliss-filled, diarrheal-discharge followed me down the hall, through the kitchen, and out the front door. I walked home and went straight to my room to await the phone call from my Uncle to my parents that I knew was coming. I lay on my bed for hours, contemplating my fate and waiting for a phone call that never came. Maybe Aunt Poster's eyes had been telling the truth, and if she'd somehow gotten me off the hook, I couldn't imagine how. I didn't come down for dinner, claiming I didn't feel well, opting instead to turn in early. Hours later, I drifted off to sleep with my last waking memory being of Aunt Poster's mesmerizing eyes and the assurance they'd given me.

Chapter Nine

I stayed away from my Uncle's place for the rest of the week, opting instead to go straight home after school to an empty house. It wasn't entirely bad because I could masturbate all I wanted without the fear of being caught, and while I took full advantage of this, something was different. I don't just mean because I was in a different place or was trying a different method of pleasuring myself or even that I was using a different hand. Something was just different now, and I couldn't quite put my finger on what it was. I still enjoyed all the masturbation, and was getting out of it exactly what I felt I needed to. It still cleared my head and cooled my loins enough to allow me to get through the day. I decided it was all in my head and tried to stroke the idea from mind, but despite my fervency, the issue still vexed me.

I hadn't seen or spoken to my Uncle or Aunt Poster since the incident, and if my parents knew, they were playing it pretty close to the vest. Maybe they were letting me stew in my own juices until I couldn't take it anymore and confessed on my own. I'd played out the beating I was certain my Dad would give me for being a pervy skeeze who jerked off in front of his own Aunt, and was convinced said beating was finally coming on Saturday morning when he announced we were going over to my Uncle's to help him install a new mirror over the sink in the bathroom. I instantly popped a ferocious fear boner upon hearing of our plan for the day, and ran to my room to take care of the matter before we had to leave. I viewed it as smoking one last cigarette before going up in front of a firing squad.

We drove even though the house was close enough to walk to, because my Dad said he didn't 'make a goddamned car payment every month for him to walk his ass around'. I sat in the passenger seat, silent until we made the final turn onto my Uncle's street.

"So . . ." I said still trying to decide what the best way to word my question. "Did he say why he's replacing the mirror? Like, did he say that something happened to the old one? Something that couldn't be fixed?"

"He didn't say," replied my Dad as he pulled into the driveway, "but you know your Uncle and his projects."

I trudged slowly behind my Dad up the walk, and kept my head down as I entered the house. I followed him down the hall, and into the kitchen where my Uncle was sitting at the table reading the paper.

"Oh, hey guys," he said cheerily. "Thanks for the help. Don't worry, this won't take long."

He set the paper aside, stood up, and motioned my Dad to follow him out onto the back porch. They were either bringing the mirror in from out there or wanted to have a minute alone to go over the plan they'd spent the week concocting on how to best punish me. I was distracted when the aroma of Aunt Poster's famous stewed bean stew filled my nostrils and my olfactory senses diverted the entirety of my working faculties to locating its origin.

Gone from my mind were thoughts of my impending punishment. I swiveled on my heels to find see the familiar big red pot boiling away on the stove. I smiled and enjoyed the fraction of a second of warmth and happiness just seeing the pot gave me, but the moment was over as soon as it had begun when I saw Aunt Poster. She was hanging off to the right side of the stove where she always does when she's cooking. I hadn't noticed her I'd first entered the kitchen, but that was understandable for how distracted I was.

Aunt Poster's eyes met mine, and although she didn't speak; they told me all I needed to know. Everything was going to be okay. I didn't know how, but that didn't matter. My fear melted away under the all-consuming aroma of Aunt Poster's stew, which I was now relaxed enough to actually enjoy. The back door swung open and in came my Dad and Uncle each holding one side of what I assumed was the new bathroom mirror, but it was covered in a heavy, padded blanket so I couldn't be sure.

"Let's go, son," said my Dad as they walked past me struggling with the awkwardness, shape, and weight distribution of the mirror. Clearly neither of them wanted to lug the bulk of the load. "Wipe that look off your face and come help. They'll be plenty of time for that stuff later."

I jumped up terrified by the ambiguity of his statement. Had he caught me staring luridly at Aunt Poster? What *stuff* was he talking about? What did he mean?

"W-what?" I stammered actually rubbing my hand across the entirety of my face.

"I know you smell your Aunt's cooking," replied my Dad, "but stop drooling and come help. There'll be plenty of time for stewed peas when we're done."

He was talking about the stew, not the creepy looks I was shooting across the room at my Aunt. He didn't know. He didn't know anything at all. I felt the blood rush to my face, and kept my head down so Aunt Poster wouldn't see me blush. I wasn't blushing from embarrassment, but from the excitement of feeling like I got away with something.

I followed my Dad and Uncle down the hall toward the bathroom not sure how exactly they wanted me to help them. There wasn't enough space between the walls in the hall to turn the mirror so all three of us could carry it, and it seemed to me like the two of them had it just fine anyway. I walked slowly behind them as they grumbled to each other while

41

moving the final few feet to the bathroom.

"Okay, put it down here," said my Uncle, already bringing his side halfway down. "Let's lean it up against the wall so I can rest a minute."

They managed to put their respective ends down at the same time and my Uncle pulled the padded blanket from the new mirror. It was a lot bigger than the old mirror, and a lot nicer too. I hoped it wasn't too expensive.

"Careful now, be careful," my Uncle spat at my Dad as they rested the lip of the mirror against the wall.

"What happened to other mirror anyway?" my Dad asked.

An audible gasp escaped my throat before I had a chance to stop it, and I started coughing to play it off. Maybe I wasn't out of the woods just yet. I was seized by the sudden fear that my Uncle actually did know what I did and was waiting for this exact moment to bust me in front of my Dad so I was present to see the horror and disappointment on his face. I held my breath as he began to speak, hoping to make myself pass out before he was through with the story.

"You know, it's the damnedest thing," said my Uncle, "and actually kind of embarrassing."

My Uncle paused, put his hands on his hips, and turned toward me, locking his eyes to mine like a deadbolt being thrown. My heart sank past the bottom of my stomach, landing somewhere halfway down my small intestines in a state of advanced digestion. I gasped again, but this time it was not audible since my voice wouldn't work at a frequency discernable to the human ear. Now the other shoe was being dropped.

My Uncle raised his arm, and gestured toward me. I saw his lips move, but all I could hear was a high-pitched ringing as my vision started blurring around the edges. I didn't need to hear him to know what he was saying though, and just as suddenly as I was slipping away I was shaken back into consciousness. My Dad had a good grip on my shoulder, and was forcibly moving me back and forth with it.

"Did you hear your Uncle? He asked you a question?"

I knew my voice would still only function in dog whistle range, so I just shook my head slowly to allow more time for my wits to return.

"I asked if you remembered earlier in the week when I sort of busted in on you in the bathroom," he repeated. "Sorry again about almost breaking the door down, but I was . . . well, I was in trouble if you know what I mean."

Had I heard this right? Was he apologizing to me? My confusion was starting to make me question my own memory, and I wondered if I had imagined it all. What kind of spell had Aunt Poster put on me with those eyes? I swallowed my voice back down to a semi-normal tone and forced out words.

"Yeah. No. I mean, what? No trouble for me."

I instantly forgot what I said, but I was pretty sure it didn't make sense anyway.

"What?" my Uncle asked.

"Are you on drugs or something, boy?" my Dad asked while trying to look me in the eyes to gauge my sobriety.

"No way!" I almost shouted. "I mean, no. I'm just tired . . . and hungry, and I keep smelling Aunt Poster's stew, and—"

"We'll all eat in a minute," my Uncle cut me off. "Let me tell your Dad the story, okay? Anyway, like I said I was in some trouble."

"What kind of trouble?" my Dad asked.

"I know what you're gonna' say already, but you know I just can't resist those tacos. I honestly think she puts some weird gypsy voodoo shit in that sauce."

"Madame Janie's strikes again," my Dad said, shaking his head with a half a curled up smirk steadily climbing the side of his face. "You know those tacos will make you sick at least three out of every five times. Why would you ever go to a gypsy taco truck? It even sounds wrong when you say those three words out loud together."

"Yeah, yeah I know," replied my Uncle. "Sheesh, if I wanted a lecture I'd go to the kitchen and get one from . . . her." My Uncle gestured with his thumb toward the kitchen as he said this, and paused immediately after listening to see if Aunt Poster had heard him. Satisfied she hadn't, he continued. "Trust me, it's worth the risk to me. Every time."

"Well, I guess that's just your business then," said my Dad.

This was a phrase my Dad used quite often. It was a catch-all, throw away kind of line for him, and he had the uncanny knack of being able to make it apply to any situation. Later in life, I would come to find he used it quite often to respond to my Mom when he wasn't paying attention to what she was saying. He was smart enough to change it to 'her business' or 'his business' depending on the context. I could tell when he really stopped caring about what she was saying when he would change it to 'their business'. I don't blame him though. My Mom could really drone on about a lot of stuff that wasn't important. I would have done the same thing if I were him. I love my Mom, but she is a horrible storyteller and an even worse conversationalist.

"Yeah, I guess it is," my Uncle retorted mockingly. "Anyway, like I said I'd thrown the dice and eaten at Madam Janie's, hence the reason for the . . . trouble I was in. I just about tore the door off the hinges to get in there, because of the direness of the situation. If I hadn't gotten in there when I did I wouldn't have just had to throw my pants away. I would have had to have the hall re-carpeted and the walls re-painted. That's how bad this was, and that was just a conservative estimate. There was potential for the damage to be much worse."

My Uncle paused here to impress upon us the seriousness of the shit he'd had to take. I guess he thought stopping the conversation would force us to picture the whole area covered in shit, and he was right, because that's exactly what we did. "So anyway, after I ran you over to get in there," he said gesturing toward me, "I sat down and let it all go. That was the last thing I remember."

"What does this have to do with the mirror?" asked my Dad. "So far, all you've told us is about how you had to take a shit and that you took it without ruining your pants or the hall."

"I'm getting there," barked my Uncle. "Like I said, reaching the point of evacuation was the last thing I remembered. The next thing I knew, I was sitting at the kitchen table with a bag of ice pressed against my forehead, my pants missing, and the little missus hanging on the wall next to me."

"What do you mean 'the last thing you remember'?" asked my Dad. "Did you pass out or something?"

"Well, sort of, I guess," he said. "Apparently the rush from the . . . release must have momentarily drained the blood from my brain and made me lose control, because I jumped up off the commode and did a header right into the mirror. Busted it to shit all over the place, but I was lucky and came out of it with only a couple small cuts."

He pointed to a few abrasions on the side of his forehead retreating back into his hairline and out of site.

"How do you know you did that if you passed out?" I piped up anxious for more details.

"Well, lucky for me, your Aunt was in the bathroom at the time doing her meditation and saw it all happen. She got me to the kitchen so she could patch me up. She even cleaned the mess."

"Your wife meditates in the bathroom and you just shit in front of her?"

I couldn't tell if my Dad was more perplexed or disgusted by this thought.

"Sure, she always does. You saw her in there, right?"

He directed the question to me, and my Dad's turned for my response, his expression twisted further by confusion. I shrugged wide-eyed, trying to seem just as confused as he was. "If she hadn't been in there who knows what could have happened. I could have bled out before anyone found me."

"You said your pants were gone when you came to. What happened with them?"

"Oh . . . well apparently I wasn't exactly finished with my business when I did the header into the mirror, which contributed heavily to the overall mess. My pants ended up having to be thrown out after all."

"Are you telling me you shit all over the bathroom? What kind of a mess are we walking into here?"

I could tell my Dad was becoming increasingly more frustrated with the situation. He'd come over to help install a mirror, not deal with a biohazard site. My Uncle opened the bathroom door wide to allow my Dad and I to look inside. Besides the mirror being completely gone, there was nothing even remotely amiss. The strong smell of bleach wafted out and burned our nostrils, but that was the only offensive thing as far as I could tell.

"I told you, my sweet angel cleaned everything up, and basically saved my life. She got every shard of glass too. I swear, I don't know what I'd do without her. I hope I never have to find out."

"I can't believe she cleaned your shitty ass up," said my Dad. "If I were your wife, I would have left you there and probably never used the bathroom again. I might have even moved out. You don't deserve a woman that good."

46

"I agree," said my Uncle. "Now let's do this thing so we can get to eating stew. That smell is starting to drive me nuts."

My Dad and Uncle picked up the mirror again, and took it into the bathroom as I followed behind, still not sure of how I was going to help. They leaned it up against the sink, and my Uncle stood back to examine the space where the new mirror would hang. I think my Dad and I noticed the pinkish-red lump protruding from the back of his head through his hair at the same time, but he spoke up first.

"Where'd you get that lump?" he asked. "I thought you hit the mirror with the front of your head?"

"You know I'm not sure," he replied, rubbing the bump as he spoke. "I just assumed I got it from the fall somehow. Who knows? Hurts like a son of a bitch though."

It was in that moment I knew exactly how he'd gotten that lump, and exactly how Aunt Poster had helped me. I was comforted and scared by the way this made me feel, but that didn't stop me from liking the feeling. I stood there watching while my Dad and Uncle argued about how to center the mirror when something caught my eye.

It was Aunt Poster hanging out in the hall across from the open bathroom door at an angle that allowed for only me to see her. We locked eyes and she winked. I winked back, and couldn't help but smile about our shared secret. The same strange and confusing feelings welled up even stronger, and smacked me in the chest over and over like an incoming tide eroding away all my doubt and fear.

Chapter Ten

I watched my Dad and Uncle install the new mirror, but that was the extent of the help I had to offer. They mostly argued about where the center of the wall was in relation to the center of the mirror until finally choosing a spot. When it was all said and done, the mirror was a good six inches left of center, but by then, neither of them cared anymore. The task had already taken longer than either of them wanted and we were all hungry.

I didn't talk much as we ate, and mostly stole glances at Aunt Poster when I could, hoping to replicate the moment we'd shared earlier. She had gone back to hanging by the stove as we ate, and no matter how many sideways glances I gave, our eyes never met. She was busying herself with other cooking tasks of course, but I thought she might look up at least once if for nothing else other than to make sure we were enjoying our stew. She kept her eyes fixed upon her task, leaving me feeling awkward and slightly rejected. That's when the doubt crept in.

What if I was confusing what Aunt Poster did to help me as something else? What if she only did what she did solely to spare me the embarrassment of having to tell the rest of the family I'd jerked off all over the bathroom while making eyes at my own Aunt? It was possible this was some kind of 'get out of jail free' card Aunt Poster was giving me in hopes I wouldn't make the same mistake twice. Perhaps this was all just her way of telling me to get my shit together, or at the very least exercise some self-control.

I cringed at the possibility that I'd read something into

the situation, and our moment never existed. Maybe it was just all in my head? The thought knotted my stomach and killed my appetite, so I rested my spoon in the bowel and stared down at my reflection in the oily green surface of its contents.

"What's wrong with you?" my Dad asked just before jamming another spoonful into his already full mouth. Multicolored flecks of bean sprayed out, and smacked against the side of my face, punctuating each syllable. "I thought you said you were hungry?"

I shook off the daze, and saw my Dad had halted the marathon procession of food into his mouth. His face began to morph into the same sideways-mouthed look of confusion he'd given my Uncle in the hall, so I acted fast before the transformation was complete.

"I am, I am," I blurted spooning stew into my face as fast as I could until my cheeks were packed to capacity and broth poured from my puckered lips like a chunky brown and green waterfall.

"Christ son, slow down," my Dad said. "You can't taste it if you eat like that. Hell, that's insulting to your Aunt, who worked hard on this stew. The least you could do is take the time to enjoy it."

He gestured toward Aunt Poster, and my head reflexively turned in the direction he pointed. She was looking at me now, but there were no quiet whispers of hidden secrets behind her eyes. Now they held the parental sternness of an adult disciplinarian siding with my Dad. Her silent scolding pierced the soaring wings of my wishful thinking to send me crashing back down to the land of logic-based reality. I turned away slowly and lowered my head as I was struck with the compiled shame comprised from all the times in my life I should have felt it but didn't.

"Sorry," I mustered, letting broth drip from my mouth

49

back into the bowl. Bits of partially chewed bean bounced off the rim to the table creating a Pollock-like aesthetic.

My Dad had already gone back to shoveling stew into his stew-hole, and my Uncle hadn't looked up to begin with, so the mess went unnoticed. I dipped my spoon into my bowl and mechanically brought it to my mouth. I had to force the stuff past my lips because it didn't taste half as good as it had seconds ago.

My Dad and Uncle got second and third helpings while I struggled to finish my first. I was vaguely aware of them talking, but the sound around me had regressed into a droning hum I had no interest in interpreting. I felt like I was drinking in rejection through my pores from the air around me. It raced through my veins and turned to lead in my heart in an attempt to stifle its beating and sink the useless organ down into my bowels. Despite the ruthless assault, my heart still beat, and refused to go down without a fight.

"Hey!" My Dad's voice came out of nowhere as his hand slapped down hard on the table in front of me, rattling the spoon from the side of my bowl. "Your Aunt asked you a question. Are you asleep or something?"

"W-what?" I choked on the final remnants from my final bite of stew.

"She asked if you wanted more," my Dad said. "Are you deaf, or asleep?"

"Oh no, I mean, no I'm not, but also . . . I don't think I want anymore."

"Well that's good, because you're not getting it anyway. We gotta' get home."

We all stood up, and my Uncle took our stacked bowls over to the sink for Aunt Poster to wash.

"Thanks for the stew, guys," my Dad said as we walked out of the kitchen.

He stopped just short of the doorway, and shot me a look

that took more than a second or two to decipher the meaning of.

"Oh," I finally said snapping to it. "Thank you for the stew."

I offered a half wave to my Uncle, but refused to look in the direction of Aunt Poster who was now hung over by the sink where water was running for the dishes. I guess it was a good enough display of gratitude for my Dad, because he was already mostly down the hall before I finished my sentence. I hurried quickly after him, and we rode home in silence. When we got there, I went to my room, and locked the door.

Chapter Eleven

As soon as the lock clicked signifying the tumbler was in place, and my privacy was ensured, I began masturbating. I masturbated long, and I masturbated hard, and all the while I refused to let myself indulge in any fantasies involving Aunt Poster. I'd built up quite a few in my mind over the week, but would not allow myself draw from the cache. Instead, I busied my mind with thoughts of girls from school, and all the mysteriously hypnotic attributes they were developing that intrigued and repulsed me at the same time. I knew they would never talk to me, but talking wasn't required for the scenarios I had in mind. Something was wrong though. I couldn't cum.

I usually came twice before I could even get my dick out of my pants, but now I suddenly had the stamina of a seasoned pro. No matter how much I thought about the bouncy, soft parts of girls, or even the non-bouncy soft parts, I could not achieve completion. Determined to overcome my plight, I tightened my grip, dug in, and started stroking harder and faster, convinced that if I could put a crack in the levee, the whole dam would eventually burst. The only thing that cracked, however, was the skin around my glans, and all that burst were tiny, crimson, blood droplets from between those cracks. It was no use.

I let go of my injured member, and fell backwards on the bed as my crotch and head throbbed in unison. As quickly as Aunt Poster had given me so much pleasure, she took it all away just as fast. I didn't believe it was possible to feel this foolish, and decided if this was how love, or whatever it is

I felt, was, then I wanted nothing to do with it. I refused to allow my mind and body to be tortured by such an abstract emotion. No, I would not be controlled by 'love' as so many fools were who'd come before me. I would be strong. I adhered to this declaration for about two minutes until thoughts of Aunt Poster forced their way into my mind, and stomped around to rouse my feelings once again.

"No," I said out loud to myself. "No, no, nope, na-uh, no, no!"

I jumped up from my bed, and accidently brushed the back of my hand against my exposed, chaffed genitalia, and crumpled to the ground under the pain. Luckily it was excruciating enough to clear my mind of Aunt Poster for a moment, but it wasn't enough to keep the thoughts fully abated. I got up from the floor, careful this time, and gingerly tucked my wounded wiener away behind the denim safety of my jeans. Suddenly, I thought of the perfect thing to keep my mind distracted from thoughts of my Aunt, and I headed across the room to my desk. I was going to do my homework.

Atop my desk were some folders, a red three-ring binder, and the only textbook I'd brought home from school for the weekend. It was my book for Shop Class. I grabbed at the pages and threw them open randomly. When I looked down, my injured dick became impossibly hard and my jeans flooded with semen that pushed through the tightly woven denim and oozed past the teeth of my zipper like Play-doh through the star-shaped Fun-Factory hole. I was hit with a multitude of orgasms at once, and I fell to the floor unable to control my limbs. The page I'd randomly opened to displayed a lesson on how to rebuild a transmission, complete with detailed pictures. The sight of it was too much for me to block out or ignore. I paid for my repression with insufferable bliss.

Just as my balls released what I thought may be the last bit of semen they'd ever produce, there was loud knock at my door followed by the jangling of the doorknob. The lock, however, remained true.

"The door's locked, son," my Dad yelled louder than necessary through the thin wood of the cheap door.

"What . . .uh, uh, uh," I stammered through shivering ecstasy. "What is it? I don't feel . . . good."

"Your Aunt is on the phone for you," he said. "I think she wants to talk to you about your manners, or lack thereof, from earlier this afternoon. I thought I told you to apologize."

I tried to answer but couldn't as a torrent of orgasms ripped through me like a high school football team through a homecoming banner. I felt torn to shreds and would need to wait until my parts grew back together before I'd be able to answer. My Dad would simply have to wait outside my door with the phone until I could achieve this. The doorknob rattled again, harder this time, and was off-putting enough to jar me out of my orgasmic hallucination.

"Just a minute Dad, sheesh," I called from the floor, suddenly clearheaded. "Let me . . . put my pants on, okay?"

"Why do you have your pants off in the middle of the day?"

I pulled myself to my feet on the side of the desk, and walked like a newborn deer across the room unbuttoning my cum-soaked jeans as I went.

"I took them off because my stomach hurt," I said peeling the moist and sticky denim down my thighs pulling patches of leg hair out at the roots. "I think Aunt Poster's stew made me sick. Maybe she's calling to apologize to *me*!"

I kicked the ruined pants into the corner; pulled on the sweatpants I usually slept in, and opened my door.

"I highly doubt that since I ate three helpings and I feel just fine," my Dad said, handing the cordless phone through the door to me. "I swear, you must have gotten your weak constitution from your Mom, because your Uncle and I never get sick. Now, apologize again to your Aunt, then get your ass out back to help me cut the lawn."

He turned and plodded down the hall, and I waited until he'd rounded the corner before bringing the phone to my ear.

"Hello?" I said meekly into the receiver.

As Aunt Poster began to speak, I knew that everything was going to be okay.

Chapter Twelve

On the phone that day, Aunt Poster said she knew what I was going through, how my body was changing, and how natural it all was. She confirmed my suspicions by telling me how she convinced my Uncle that he'd destroyed the bathroom in his gypsy-taco induced shit-fit, so I wouldn't have to feel embarrassed or ashamed. I didn't tell her that shame was almost impossible for me to feel, at least where masturbation was concerned. I didn't want to tell her just yet that I'd only recently experienced the emotion as a reaction to my quickly developing feelings for her.

She said she noticed I hadn't come over after school since the incident, and encouraged me to come back. She said she had a plan to help me through both my emotional and physical changes through a mentoring of sorts. All I had to do was stop by after school, and she would act as my 'guide through the choppy waters of adolescence'. Aunt Poster liked to use weird-ass mixed metaphors like that, which my Uncle once told me was a byproduct of all her yoga training. If anyone asked, she said she would tell people she was teaching me beginner's yoga.

I know my Uncle loved Aunt Poster, but for some reason, he was not at all into the practice of yoga she was so passionate about. He supported her in it, which was obvious from the time and energy he put into creating a small studio for her in the house, but other than that he wanted nothing to do with it. I didn't have to worry about telling my parents anything since they were both at work for several hours after I was out of school, and assumed I stopped by my Aunt and

Uncle's daily anyway.

When Monday came, the first day I was to meet with Aunt Poster to begin my life training, I was a nervous and horny wreck. This wasn't too much of a departure from how I always felt, but now these familiar feelings seemed to hold more weight than usual, and I was being crushed beneath them. Before I left school, I masturbated twice in the boys room on the far east side of the building, then on my way out, I stopped off at the bathroom on the far west side to beat another one off for good measure. I'd made a promise to myself that I wouldn't jerk off at school, but I'd broken that commitment after only a day and a half.

I took the long way to Aunt Poster's even though I was beyond excited to get there. My initial motivation was to have more time to prepare myself mentally, but I realized I didn't know what I was preparing for, or even how to go about that preparation. That's when I decided to start running, which was a bad idea because I was horribly out of shape and was a panting, sweaty mess by the time I got there. I bent over holding my knees, wheezing, and dry heaved a few times into the bushes. Nothing came up, but I could taste the thin layer of bile as it coated my mouth and throat, and my attempts to spit the flavor away were less than successful.

I'm not sure if it was the muscles contracting in my stomach from the heaving that brought it on, or my jeans rubbing against my crotch as I ran, but I was seized by the compulsion to masturbate one more time before entering the house. I took a look behind me, and determined the bushes would provide an adequate amount of coverage. My fingers danced around my crotch working to unfasten my button, and yank down my zipper as I began to swell behind it. I took one last look over my shoulder before committing fully to the tug-fest, but just as I unleashed my beast I heard a tinkling sound from the porch in front of me. Through the bushes I saw Aunt Poster hung to the right of the front door above the small round table flanked by the two chairs that were always on the porch. They were white, rattan, and hideous, but my Uncle swore up and down that they were 'antiques,' and 'a great find,' even though they looked like they were salvaged from a sunken cruise liner in the eighties. The tinkling sound came from the melting ice cubes swirling around a tall glass of Aunt Poster's famous lemonade sitting in the middle of the table.

I didn't know how long she'd been there, but she could clearly see me. I tried to turn away and jam my wilting schlong back in my pants, but I lost my balance and fell dick first into the front lawn. If the neighbors were watching, there was certainly nothing to obscure their view now. I sprung back up clumsily, fixed my pants, and whirled around just in time to hear the screen door clang shut. Aunt Poster was gone, but the lemonade remained, and now there was a red and white striped straw perched in the middle maintaining its balance between two of the larger ice cubes. I could see, even from the lawn, that it wasn't any regular straw, but the extra-wide kind that typically accompanied milkshakes.

My excitement trumped my embarrassment and I tripped up the steps to the porch toward the lemonade. I snatched the slick, condensation-covered glass and slurped greedily from the straw, downing half the contents in one tremendous gulp. There was obviously something different about this lemonade, and I wondered why Aunt Poster would deviate from her perfect recipe. It burned like I'd swallowed a spoonful of fire ants that were biting their way down to my stomach before being melted alive by my digestive juices.

Due to the wideness of this particular straw, I'd already sucked in the second half before I could process the difference. I was only seventeen, but I knew what whiskey tasted like from taking the final swig of the bottles my Dad would empty while telling stories in the garage. He was far too drunk by then to realize I'd stolen the final sip. Why would Aunt Poster put whiskey in my lemonade? Was she trying to get me drunk?

I dropped the glass and it shattered on the wooden planks of the porch, sending the mostly melted ice cubes off into the sunlight and to their demise. The red and white striped straw, albeit wider than normal, wasn't wide enough to keep from disappearing through the space between two of the porch planks. I coughed madly, unsure whether my lungs or the contents of my stomach would be ejected first. Luckily, the spastic fit resulted in nothing more than lightheadedness, a sore solar plexus, and a slight tinge of horniness, which I used to urge myself on. That, along with the bolstered confidence and euphoria I was feeling from the special lemonade, proved more than enough to turn me on my heels, and send me through the door.

The screen door slammed with a screeching clang behind me. I closed the front door by kicking the wood block my Aunt and Uncle used to prop it open when the weather was mild. It was darker than normal in the house, and despite being familiar with the layout I allowed time for my eyes to adjust so I wouldn't be surprised by anything. Seeing Aunt Poster on the porch without knowing how long she'd been watching had me on higher alert than normal. When I could see, it didn't look like anything was out of place or amiss, and I scanned the walls several times for Aunt Poster, but she was nowhere to be seen.

I heard something come from the living room, so I stepped lightly down the hall to investigate. All of the shades were drawn, which was not usually the case in the middle of the day, and it made the living room even darker than the hall. My eyes didn't need further adjusting though, because there was a single candle lit by the swinging door that lead to Aunt Poster's makeshift yoga studio. The door was still swinging as if recently used.

I stepped into the room, and although my foot found solid purchase on the soft carpet, my balance faltered. I caught myself on the arm of the couch as a thick and loud thrumming rocked from the back of my head, to the front, then to the back again. I burped up a mouthful of burning lemonade, and quickly swallowed it back down. I all of a sudden felt woozy, and the sight of the couch made me very badly want to be accepted into its comforting embrace where I would slip out of consciousness. The flicker of the candle caught my eye again though, and gave me the presence of mind I needed to cut through the fog and carry on.

I walked across the room slowly in order to keep my balance, using the candlelight as a beacon to guide my way. I paused at the door unsure of what to expect, but I was strangely relaxed and ready for whatever was about to happen. I had to give credit for my courage to the lemonade, because without its numbing effect, I would have most certainly not proceeded.

I pushed open the door, and peeked in. The room would have been the darkest of all if it weren't for all the candles placed precariously throughout the makeshift yoga studio. My nose was assaulted with jasmine, lilac, rose petal, and vanilla from the combined scents they gave off, but the mixture wasn't offensive to me. I stepped through the door, allowing it to swing shut behind me, and scanned the walls for Aunt Poster.

She hung basking in the strong concentration of candlelight. Something was different though. Aunt Poster had a drastic application of makeup. It wasn't gaudy, just unfamiliar to me. Her eyes were perfectly outlined with sharp, dramatic points, like a cat. I'd heard the term 'smoky eyes' and 'smoldering eye shadow,' but never actually understood what they meant until this moment. Her lips were the exact reddish pink of the inside of a ripe strawberry. Her coy smile punctuated the allure of the shade.

Her makeup was so intrinsically intoxicating to me, that it took longer than it should have to realize she was wearing nothing but fishnet pantyhose. Aunt Poster remained silent as she faced away from me, went into the downward dog pose, and beckoned with her eyes for me to step up behind her. The thrumming in my head stopped, the fog lifted, and I could think clearly once again.

Chapter Thirteen

By the time I stumbled out of the house the sun had long since taken its leave, and the street lights had been burning for the better part of an hour already. The broken glass was still on the porch. I stepped over it and onto the steps. I wasn't sure why my Uncle wasn't home yet, but I suspected Aunt Poster was somehow responsible for his tardiness. I dug my hands in my pockets, strolled across the lawn, and set out toward home. The night was cool and it felt good to walk, so I took the long way again, but didn't feel the need to run this time. I strolled with a gait more leisurely than ever, using the added time to process my recent experience.

It was almost too new. Too fresh to truly deal with or make sense of. Still, like a newly formed scab, it begged for me to pick and poke at it. It wasn't that my brain was too underdeveloped to understand either. It was quite developed in fact. Adept at picking apart abstract thought. It was my personality and sensibility that suffered from lack of development due to immaturity, which I clung to with a death grip, afraid of what might happen if I let go. None of this stopped me from running a constant replay of the afternoon's events on repeat in my mind for the whole walk home. I was so absorbed in mentally reliving the experience that I didn't notice my Uncle's car was in the driveway as I walked up the lawn and through the front door.

"There he is, and not a moment too soon," said my Uncle to me from the kitchen table where he sat drinking coffee with my parents.

To say the combination of his voice and presence were

disquieting to me in that moment would be an understatement. I responded only with stunned silence while fumbling to pull my hands from my pockets.

"Your Aunt told me she was gonna' give it to you, but I didn't think it would take this long," he said.

If there would have been a way for me to devour myself from the inside and disappear from sight, I wouldn't have been able to do it fast enough in this particular moment. What was this? Did Aunt Poster tell them what happened, or rather what she was going to do to me? I wanted to force myself to faint as a temporary relief from reality, but I unfortunately could not will myself unconscious so I continued staring blankly.

"Are you hungry?" my Mom asked, standing up from the table and crossing toward me. "I bet you worked up quite an appetite over there, or did your Aunt make you eat before you left?"

What was my Mom even asking me right now? Was this a loaded question? She kissed me on my forehead, and continued on to the counter where she freshened her coffee.

"You don't feel very warm," she said while absently spooning sugar. "I thought you'd be nice and sweaty with all Aunt Poster had in store for you."

Could it be true that my own mother knew of the deplorable and depraved things I'd done with Aunt Poster? Or more accurately, the things Aunt Poster did with me? Did to me? Now I started sweating, and was about to come completely unhinged, when my Dad stood up and gestured sternly at me with his coffee cup.

"I hope all those chores Aunt Poster had you do today taught you a lesson about manners and being appreciative."

Chores? Lesson? I was certainly appreciative, that was true. All of a sudden I was able to see Aunt Poster's grand plan. The reason she was able to keep my Uncle away from the house, and keep my own family from worrying, was to tell them all she was having me do chores as a punishment. More so, she wanted to handle it herself to show she did not require the male presence of my Uncle to dole out punishment. The last part had more to do with Aunt Poster being a progressive thinker her entire life than it had to do with anything else, but that was just her style.

"Oh . . . yeah," I finally mustered running my hand back and forth through my hair to stall. "Chores are . . . done, and good."

"And did you learn your lesson?" my Mom chimed in again.

I learned a lesson all right, but I don't think it was the kind she thought I was learning.

"Yes ma'am," I rattled off, anxious to get out of the conversation.

"Good. Now, are you hungry or did you eat out your Aunt?"

Surely I didn't hear that.

"I said did you eat with your Aunt?"

Thankfully I'd imagined it, which was further indication that I needed to get the hell out of the kitchen.

"Yes," I snapped. "I mean yes ma'am. You know, I'm pretty beat. I think I'm gonna turn in early."

"I'm going to go ahead and get out of here myself," said my Uncle, pushing away from the table leaving his empty coffee cup for my Mom to deal with. "I hope you left enough for me, sport!"

He elbowed my ribs playfully as he passed by, and I shuddered at the implications of his statement, unbeknownst to him or anyone else in the room. "Are you sure you don't want anything before . . ."

"No, I 'm fine, Mom. Goodnight!"

I cut her off before she could ask another cringe-worthy

question, turned on my heels, and shot up the stairs to my room. I closed the door, turned off the lights, and lay back on my bed to think. I heard my Uncle's car start in the driveway, the sound of AM talk radio chatter spilling from his ever-cracked open windows. As he backed out of the driveway, his headlights flashed across the front of the house, momentarily illuminating my room, making my pile of dirty clothes cast an evil looking shadow across the wall. The hum of his engine faded out as he drove up the street and around the corner on his way back to his house. Back to Aunt Poster.

The thought of her sent waves of overwhelming joy and grueling anguish crashing down on me, spawning conflicting thoughts from both ends of the spectrum. I knew I was young and I knew I didn't have the life experience to understand love and relationships, but as far as I knew, I was in love with Aunt Poster. She had to love me back too, or else why would she have . . . taught me all the lessons she did tonight? On the other hand, she was my Aunt and she was married to my Uncle. How could she be in love with me and be married to him? I loved my Uncle too, and I respected the man, even though my actions as of late might not have reflected that.

I knew my Uncle was pretty stupid, and nowhere near the caliber of man Aunt Poster needed or deserved, but he was still my Uncle after all. I owed him an explanation because he deserved one. He deserved to know that his seventeen-year-old nephew just balled his wife a new honey-hole. Maybe those weren't the best words to put it in, but something along those lines. The important thing was to tell him what I did, and that Aunt Poster and I were in love, and there was nothing he could do about it. I'd have plenty of time to figure out exactly how I wanted to put it on the walk back over there.

I pulled the brakes on my train of thought, derailing it entirely as it screeched to a messy halt. What was I thinking?

I didn't need to tell my Uncle how I felt. I needed to tell Aunt Poster. Even though I knew that she knew, I felt like I needed to say it. I needed to say that a look from her alone was enough to show me the insignificance of every single thing I deemed problematic. My insecurities deflated and shriveled beneath her touch, and her love had changed me into a man. I realized I'd made the transformation only a couple of hours ago, but that didn't make it any less important. I needed to tell Aunt Poster these things, and I needed to tell her right now. My Uncle was the least important part of this equation to me, so he'd have to wait in line to get an earful of what my heart had to say.

I got out of bed, went to the window, and slowly raised it to keep from making any noise. I climbed out and onto the eave that hung over the front door, then slid down the drainpipe to the yard. It was a maneuver I'd perfected years ago but hadn't used lately since I no longer had to sneak out to go places at night. I only did it now so that I wouldn't have to answer any questions from my parents on the way out. I dashed through the yard and hit the sidewalk running. This time, I didn't take the long way.

Chapter Fourteen

I stopped running when I got to my Aunt and Uncle's block, and walked the rest of the way. I wanted to catch my breath so I could go in guns blazing and say what I had to say instead of throwing up, and/or jerking off in the bushes out front. I tried to organize my thoughts as best I could so I'd sound halfway intelligent, but my emotions were running far too high to allow for that sort of focus. I decided to stop over-thinking it because this was about love and passion, and you weren't supposed to think when you talked about those things. You were supposed to speak from your heart, and just let it all out. At least that's the way I assumed it was supposed to be since I had no real experience to draw from.

I was three houses away when my stomach started churning like a busted septic tank, and the familiar taste of bile crept up my throat to let my tongue know what to expect. I stopped for a second to clutch at my gut and take some deep breaths. I was terrified out of my mind. I was about to tell the woman I loved exactly how I felt about her, and then immediately turn around to her husband, who is also my Uncle, and tell him what I told her. That, and how just hours ago Aunt Poster had taken my hand with a gentle delicateness and ushered me across the bridge to manhood, coaxing the rapidity of my 'coming of age' with her spellbinding stare.

I swallowed hard to choke back the sick rising from my gut and willed my nerves away with deep breaths. After the third deep breath, my stomach bucked with all its might, and I retched into the gutter under the streetlight. I didn't have much in me to throw up, but evacuating the small amount of bright yellow bile was enough to set me straight again. I was still terror-struck and anxiety-ridden, but at least I knew I wouldn't throw up again. Probably. I straightened, wiped my mouth on the back of my hand, and smoothed the front of my shirt. My Uncle's house was only fifteen more feet down the sidewalk. Each step felt like I was moving only inches at a time. I imagined this was how ancient beasts felt when struggling to walk through deadly tar pits, and I hoped I wasn't headed for the same fate as them.

I heard what sounded like a cross between a cat in heat, and another cat in heat that had also been hit by a car. Once I was past the neighbor's shrubs enough to see the familiar front porch, I learned my guess was decidedly off the mark. The sound was my Uncle wailing while sitting on the porch steps with his head in his hand. His other hand hung over his knee with a piece of paper dangling from between his thumb and forefinger. This was not what I expected to see, and I was instantly knocked off track from my intended course of action. Suddenly, what I had to say about whatever it was I thought I was feeling didn't seem so urgent and important when held up against the actual suffering of my Uncle. He was so loud he didn't hear me walk up the lawn, and I stood awkwardly in front of him for a moment before I spoke.

"Hey . . . what's . . . uh . . . wrong?'

I'd lost any eloquence I possessed as I stood in front of my damaged Uncle, heartache incarnate. He looked through eyes as red and swollen as some of the more tender spots on Aunt Poster after we were through, but I pushed the distracting thought from my mind before it fully developed. My Uncle didn't answer, but instead made a weak groan while looking down at the paper pinched between his fingers. I didn't need to see the paper to know what it said, or at least the gist, but I still reached out to take it from him. He gladly relinquished it to me, and pulled his hand back as if he were passing off hazardous materials. In a way, I guess he was. I held the paper up, and moved over to catch the light from the porch so I could read while he continued to moan.

I was right about the note, but that didn't keep my heart from cracking down the center, and doing a swan dive down into my stomach to wait for its chance to escape during my next vomit episode. She was gone. According to her note, Aunt Poster said she would always love my Uncle, but she found herself becoming emotionally unavailable due to a 'great deal of confusion' she was experiencing regarding her 'path in life'. Apparently she was going off to meditate in the mountains on a retreat, and then planned to finally open her own yoga studio. It was her hope that these things would help her to align with happiness and be content.

It read like hippie, new age speak for: *you're holding me back, so fuck off!* Speaking of fucking off, there was no mention of me in the note at all. I turned it over to check the back, and then scanned through the front again to make sure I hadn't missed my name, but it was not included. My eyes started to tear up, and I feared my next vomit episode was to occur presently. I looked up from the paper to my Uncle, who was now clutching his knees with his head down, sobbing loudly into his own lap. I too was crying, but stifled my sobs while tears ran saline trails that stood out like strips of reflector tape down my reddened cheeks. I could see the shards of shattered glass on the porch behind my Uncle, who was undoubtedly sitting on some of them. I stared transfixed by the bits of glass glittering in the porch light. It reminded me of all the flickering candle flames that were burning in Aunt Poster's yoga studio, the passion of our deeds burning along with them. It bothered me that she hadn't cleaned up the glass before she left, but I wasn't sure why it did. "Gone," my Uncle finally managed to say, raising his head enough to peer over his knees at me through the tear-flooded pits of bunched up, raw, red flesh that were his eye sockets. "She's just gone."

Now my Uncle looked at me as if he'd just snapped to the fact that I was standing right in front of him. He sat up straight, and wiped the back of his arm across his snotty, wet face.

"You," he said. "You were just here. What are you doing here now? Did she say anything to you? Was she acting strange? What do you know? Do you hear me? What do you know?"

My Uncle bounded up from the steps, grabbed me by the shoulders, and shook my thin frame like he was trying to make a martini from my bodily fluids. I couldn't answer, so I just cried. He shook me, and I cried, and he shook me some more until I could finally push words past the jagged lump in my throat.

"I don't know!" I yelled. "I don't know! I don't know anything . . . but I wish I did!"

This wasn't a total lie. I really didn't know anything about her leaving, and it wouldn't be right of me to assume what happened between us had anything to do with it, no matter how bad I wanted it to be the reason. My own adolescent, malformed bravado made me want to think that she didn't leave because of me, but for me. I knew this wasn't a productive way to think in this moment, or even in general, but I couldn't help it. The thought burned through my brain, pushed its way through the roof of my mouth, and landed on my tongue scolding me into speaking against my will.

"Was there another note for me?" I blurted out regretful of my phrasing before I'd finished the question.

"What? Note for *you*? Why would there be a note for you? You do know something, don't you? Tell me! Tell me what you know about all of this!"

He'd stopped shaking, but held my shoulders tight staring through sad, bleary eyes waiting for an answer I didn't know how to give. Instead, I just kept crying and shaking my head. Just then, headlights passed us and lit up the front yard as a car swung into the driveway. We both turned to look, and even through my own haze of tears I could see the car belonged to my parents. I blinked my eyes clear, and saw the perplexed looks on their faces through the windshield as they took in what I imagined was an awkward scene. They jumped from the car with the engine still running, and my Uncle loosened his grip letting his arms fall to his side.

"Son, what are you doing here?" My Dad shouted from the driveway.

"Dear, turn off the car and lower your voice," my Mom said to him. "You'll wake up the whole neighborhood!"

Now free of my Uncle's grip, I turned around to face my parents as they quickly closed the green gap of lawn between us in just a few wide strides. I opened my mouth to at least attempt an answer, but before I could muster a word, a shrill moan sliced a jagged line of misery through the night behind me. I turned back around to see my Uncle in mid ghastly wail with his head in his hands weeping again. I felt my parent's approach and tensed, but they blew right past me to get to my Uncle. They both hugged him. My Mom first and then my Dad, whose embrace was less than half as long as hers.

That's when I started crying again too. I couldn't help it, but nobody even noticed. My parents turned my Uncle around, and lead him up the porch steps toward the front door. They stood on either side of him, guiding with an arm apiece wrapped around his back. My Dad held the screen door open with his free hand, and it slammed hard behind them as they disappeared inside. I couldn't help but think how just hours earlier I had followed Aunt Poster through that same door, and it had slammed the same way. I wiped my face with the back of my arm, and stood there staring at the door until it was suddenly thrown back open from the inside. My Dad emerged onto the moonlit porch, and pointed at me.

"What are you waiting for?" he asked. "Get your ass in here!"

He turned around, and went back in, leaving the distinct impression that my presence inside was mandatory. I headed across the lawn slowly with my head down and shoulders slumped like I was walking to my own execution. I half expected a neighbor to throw up their window and call out *dead man walking* as I slunk the rest of the way down my own personal green mile. Shards of broken glass crunched beneath my feet as I stepped onto the porch, and I paused to look down. It had happened that afternoon, but it felt like a hundred years ago. I kicked at a larger chunk and sent it skidding across the wood planks sparkling in the porch light until going over the edge into the rose bushes. I could hear more sobbing, and my Mom and Dad consoling him as I stood there staring through the screen door.

I was going to have to tell them. There was no way around it that I could see. A moment that meant so much was in an instant marred, and forever changed by anguish and absence. I took one last deep breath, opened the screen door, and stepped inside, prepared to give my full confession.

Chapter Fifteen

I never ended up giving my *full confession* as planned, but not from lack of trying. Well, sort of. I marched into the kitchen ready to belt out loud and proud that Aunt Poster and I had made love! Not only that we were *in* love as well, which I was certain was the reason for her hasty departure. I also had a feeling she would come back soon, only it would be for me, and not my Uncle. Like I said, I was prepared to say this, but when I stepped into the kitchen I couldn't get a word in edgewise.

My Uncle's uncontrollable sobbing turned into uncontrollable hyperventilating, which had my Mom riffling through drawers looking for a paper bag while my Dad just said the word 'breathe' over and over again to his brother. Each time he said it louder than the last as if my Uncle's hearing was deteriorating by the second. Just before my Dad reached a full shout, my Mom crossed back to the table with a paper bag in one hand and a glass of water in the other. She attempted to hold the bag to my Uncle's lips for him, but he snatched it away and began puffing emphatically into it. A minute later, he let the bag drop, sat back down at the table, and chugged the entire glass of water. I thought this might be my chance, but my Dad started talking before I could.

"Breathe, okay. Just breathe," he said in a normal speaking voice this time. "Breathe, and then tell us exactly what happened."

Both of my parents must have suddenly become aware of my presence in the room, because they turned to me simultaneously and in unison signaled with their eyes for me to sit down on the stool next to the refrigerator. The intensity of their combined expressions let me know non-compliance wasn't an option, so I decided to take a seat, bide my time, and speak when the moment was right.

My Uncle began to pour his heart out to my Mom and Dad, and I started to realize that moment might never come as his harsh truths eclipsed my wishful fantasy. Apparently, my Uncle called my parents in a panic after finding the note, which was why they rushed over. The reason for my presence had yet to be brought up, but I imagined at this point it didn't matter.

It turned out my Uncle's relationship with Aunt Poster had been far from ideal for quite a while, but he'd never given up hope that they could get back to where they started. Aunt Poster didn't share in that same hope as was evident by her actions. It seemed I wasn't the first in what turned out to be a parade of infidelities Aunt Poster engaged in, and my Uncle knew about all of them. All of them except the most recent one. I listened despondently as he went into detail on each encounter describing scene after scene, each one startlingly similar to my own. Aunt Poster's yoga studio was more of a den of sexual pleasures than a place of meditative reflection.

My Uncle went on to say how he'd pleaded with her after the first time he caught her, as well as every other time to please stop. He begged her to stop. He begged her to tell him what he needed to do to make her happy. He was willing to change for her, to be the person she could love again. The person she would love again. I realized how insignificant my experience was with Aunt Poster. The feelings she'd stirred up in me were just a droplet compared to the ocean of emotions my Uncle had from a twenty-year marriage.

My confession would only further convolute the situation and pollute that ocean to an overly toxic level.

The damage caused by my selfish act could potentially tear our entire family apart, and I knew I was too fragile to endure something like that. So, I sat on the stool silently with my head down, unable to bring myself to make eye contact with my Uncle as he continued to vomit the things he'd been holding in for years all over my parents, who were blindsided, but decidedly not surprised. I would come to find out later from overhearing conversations between them that they suspected Aunt Poster's wandering ways for some time.

Several hours later, my Uncle was finally emotionally depleted, and my parents had to help him to his bed where he continued to weep softly until falling asleep. My Mom insisted we all spend the night, afraid of what my Uncle might do to himself if he woke up to an empty house. My Dad's only comment was that his brother would never do something like that, but he didn't protest us staying.

They took the spare bedroom while I was left to the living room couch with an afghan Aunt Poster had knitted years ago. I couldn't sleep, of course, and spent the night staring at the spot on the wall where Aunt Poster hung when we watched T.V. together. I spent the last few hours before dawn going through the process of divorcing myself from the feelings I'd developed for Aunt Poster. By the time the sun's first rays invaded the living room through a crack in the drapes, I was on my way to putting my short-lived idea of a relationship with my Aunt behind me.

Chapter Sixteen

The following weeks after Aunt Poster left were hard on me, but much harder on my Uncle. I suffered silently while he relied heavily on the emotional support of my parents, and to a lesser extent, myself. The three of us took turns spending the night with him to help keep him occupied, and his thoughts off of his misery. My Mom made dozens of meals for him, which she jammed into his freezer to make sure he was eating. It was a difficult time to navigate emotionally for both of us, but after a few months, things started to get better, and happiness was slowly returning to my Uncle.

He hardly mentioned Aunt Poster anymore, and had even begun the process of dismantling her 'yoga studio' and turning it into the game room he told me he always wanted. On the nights I spent with him, we would work on putting the room together until we both got tired, ate pizza, and played videogames well into the night. A little while after that, he even started dating again, and while he wasn't very forthcoming with information concerning his new love life, he seemed much happier than he'd been in years.

He went on a camping trip in early fall with someone who he referred to as 'a friend,' and I watched his house while he was away. The game room was long since finished, and although it in no way resembled the yoga studio, I still couldn't help but picture it that way as I stood in the doorway, remembering a night that now almost didn't seem real. I stayed out of the game room while he was gone, and kept the door closed so as not to be tempted into remembering. It was a long and lonely battle for me to close the door on that memory, and I suffered in silence by myself. The last thing I wanted was to peer through the keyhole and have to start all over again.

A week later, when my Uncle got home he told me to make sure I stopped by right after school, because he had something very important to share with me. I figured that, along with the money he gave me to house sit, he'd probably brought back some cool souvenirs for me, or maybe he'd finally bit the bullet and picked up the tabletop Ms. Pacman arcade game we'd both been coveting for the game room.

When I walked up the lawn that afternoon my Uncle was sitting on the porch waiting for me, drinking a tall glass of what looked like lemonade. It triggered a memory that made me physically flinch, but I pushed it down and buried it under the useless minutia I stored in my mind for just such occasions. My Uncle smiled wide when he saw m, and stood up, still holding the glass.

"Hey, there he is," he said jovially. "Thanks again for taking care of the house while I was gone, and for tidying up. The place looked great when I got in last night."

"No problem," I said smiling back, and keeping my line of vision from dipping down to the lemonade glass. "It was a nice break from Mom and Dad."

"Oh yeah, I hear that," he said playfully ruffling my hair with his free hand. "Come on inside. I've got some big news to share."

I wasn't sure if I'd classify getting a Ms. Pacman machine as 'big news,' but maybe he was trying to purposely throw me off so I'd be more surprised. I followed him in, and instead of going to the game room, we went to the kitchen where he refilled his glass.

"Did you want something to drink?" he asked. "I just made this lemonade fresh earlier this afternoon."

"Uh . . . no thanks," I said as I momentarily tasted the

acrid burning of the 'special' lemonade I'd had months ago.

I swallowed the ghost-flavor from my mouth as my Uncle returned the pitcher to the refrigerator.

"Suit yourself," he said taking a long swig from his glass. "Okay, so now for the big news. Follow me!"

Once again I figured we were heading for the game room, and once again I was wrong. I followed my Uncle out of the kitchen, down the hall, and to the bathroom where the door was closed. My Uncle paused and turned around to face me.

"Okay," he began, "I know I've been a mess for a while now, and that it's really taken a toll on you and your Mom and Dad, but I want you to know how much I appreciate you being here for me. I don't think I could've gotten through it without you guys."

I nodded intently as a thorny vine of guilt wrapped around my spine and squeezed like a prickly python. I bore the pain straight-faced as I'd practiced many times before.

"Well, I want you to know everything's going to be a-okay from now on," he continued. "I want you to meet someone."

With that he opened the door to reveal the empty bathroom. I peered past him with a confused look that he quickly picked up on.

"In here," he said walking to the closed shower curtain, and gesturing for me to come to him.

My Uncle threw open the curtain triumphantly like a bullfighter pulling his red cape away at the last second to reveal a shower just as empty as the bathroom. I scanned the small space top to bottom and left to right, but still didn't see what he was talking about until he pointed where he wanted my eyes to go. There, hanging from a hook on the shower caddy that housed shampoo, body wash, and other shower essentials was a pink, cylindrical loofa covered in glistening water droplets as evidence of recent use. I'd never used a loofa myself, but it looked similar to the one my Mom had hanging in her shower. Rough, craggy, nooks and crannies folded over each other again and again to make up the mass necessary to rip and peel away dead skin as it was designed to do. I looked back to my Uncle still confused.

"This is your new Aunt," he said beaming as he looked from her to me. "We got married on our camping trip. This is your Aunt Loofa!"

An unfamiliar feeling washed over me as he said this that stung at the same time it soothed. I would come later to know this feeling as closure. Aunt Poster was not only gone and not coming back, but also she'd been replaced. I knew presently wasn't the best time to deal with this strange new feeling, so I instead forced an overly huge smile that rivaled my Uncle's.

"Oh wow," I said enthusiastically. "That's great! I'm so happy for you, I mean, for the two of you!"

I looked back and forth between the two of them brandishing my cheesy, faux smile. My Uncle continued to look lovingly at his new bride, and caressed his fingers down her side, wiping away diamond-like water drops in the process.

"We'd been seeing each other for a few weeks before we went camping, and while we were out there we just decided what the heck, let's do this thing. No sense in waiting when you know it's right."

I nodded emphatically in agreement hoping my Uncle couldn't see through my insincerity, but he was clearly blinded by the swirling power of new love. He closed the shower curtain, and I followed him out of the bathroom. He closed the door behind him, and put his fingers to his lips to indicate quiet.

"She needs to rest now," he whispered. "We've been celebrating our nuptials for most of the day, and she's pretty worn out if you know what I mean."

He chuckled and elbowed me in the ribs before heading down the hall back to the kitchen. After that, my Uncle called my parents and invited them over for dinner under the same auspice of having 'big news' he wanted to share with them. He told them I was already there, and for them to head over as soon as they could.

They showed up half an hour later, and were taken through the same reveal I had experienced upon my arrival. Both of my parents reacted with large displays of excitement and happiness for him, but I could tell they were just as put on as mine had been. I knew that my Dad especially was reserving his actual judgment for the ride home with my Mom, but I did feel a sense of relief between the two of them that babysitting my Uncle would now be a thing of the past.

We sat down to a dinner filled with an almost overpowering joy my Uncle exuded as he regaled us with stories of the camping trip he'd just been on, along with loads of personal anecdotes about Aunt Loofa. They shared an endless list of commonalities, and had originally met at an antique shop in town where he'd purchased a vintage version of *Battleship* for the game room. He said he knew from that moment they were meant to be together, but he still took his time courting her to not seem too eager. It was on the camping trip they both confessed the strong feelings they had for each other, and the rest was history.

My parents never discussed with me their true feelings about the relationship but I imagine they talked about it at length behind closed doors as they waited for the other shoe to drop. The other shoe, however, never did drop, and as time passed, I could see their acceptance and confidence in my Uncle's new relationship. That same acceptance came harder for me, but it did eventually indeed come as I got to know Aunt Loofa. She was a better match for my Uncle than

Aunt Poster ever was, and ultimately his happiness was the most important thing.

I never developed a relationship with Aunt Loofa like I had with Aunt Poster though, and neither did I have any intention to. She didn't stir the same feelings and emotions up in me, which I counted as a blessing because I couldn't bear any additional silent suffering. She would hang in the shower whenever I used it, but my Uncle assured me it wouldn't be weird since she had been a school nurse at one time. Still, I always showered quickly, and avoided eye contact with her.

We never heard from Aunt Poster again, not that I ever expected we would, but as much as I repressed my feelings, she still held a special place in my heart. She wasn't a bad person. She was just unhappy, and had tried to handle it as best she could until she couldn't anymore. Still, though, every time I pass a yoga studio or a transmission shop, a flicker of fire from the brief flame of passion we shared flares in my loins, and I jerk one off in honor of the woman who led me by the hand into manhood.

John Wayne Comunale lives in Houston, TX, where he wiles away the days writing ridiculous stories and milking nuts for the greater good. He is a writer for the comedic collective, MicroSatan, and contributes creative non-fiction for the theatrical art group, BooTown. When he's not doing that, he tours with the punk rock disaster: johnwayneisdead . He is the author of The Porn Star Retirement Plan, and writer/illustrator of the comic-zine: The Afterlife Adventures of johnwayneisdead. John Wayne is an American actor who died in 1979.

The New Bizarro Author Series

2009-2010
Carnageland by D.W. Barbee
Naked Metamorphosis by Eric Mays
Sex Dungeon for Sale by Patrick Wensink
Rotten Little Animals by Kevin Shamel

2010-2011
How to Eat Fried Furries by Nicole Cushing
Muscle Memory by Steve Lowe
Felix and the Sacred Thor by James Steele
Love in the Time of Dinosaurs by Kirsten Alene
Uncle Sam's Carnival of Copulating Inanimals
    by Kirk Jones
The Egg Said Nothing by Caris O'Malley
Bucket of Face by Eric Hendrixson

2011-2012
A Hollow Cube is a Lonely Space by S.D. Foster
Lepers and Mannequins by Eric Beeny
Party Wolves in My Skull by Michael Allen Rose
Seven Seagulls for a Single Nipple
    by Troy Chambers
Gigantic Death Worm by Vince Kramer
The Placenta of Love by Spike Marlowe
Trashland A Go-Go by Constance Ann Fitzgerald
The Crud Masters by Justin Grimbol

2012-2013
Gutmouth by Gabino Iglesias
Avoiding Mortimer by J.W. Wargo

Her Fingers by Tamara Romero
Kitten by G. Arthur Brown
Janitor of Planet Anilingus
    by Andrew Wayne Adams
House Hunter S.T. Cartledge

2013-2014
The Mondo Vixen Massacre by Jamie Grefe
The Cheat Code for God Mode by Andy De Fonseca
Babes in Gangland by Bix Skahill
8-bit Apocalypse by Amanda Billings
Grambo by Dustin Reade
There's No Happy Ending by Tiffany Scandal
The Church of TV as God by Daniel Vlasaty

2014-2015
SuperGhost by Scott Cole
Pax Titanus by Tom Lucas
Deep Blue by Brian Auspice

2015-2016
King Space Void by Anthony Trevino
Rainbows Suck by Madeleine Swann
Arachnophile by Betty Rocksteady
Benjamin by Pedro Proenca
Rock 'n' Roll Head Case by Lee Widener
Slasher Camp for Nerd Dorks by Christoph Paul
Elephant Vice by Chris Meekings
Pixiegate Madoka by Michael Sean Le Sueur
Towers by Karl Fischer

2016-2017
Guitar Wolf by Nicholaus Patnaude
Hate From the Sky by Sean M. Thompson
Aunt Post by John Wayne Comunale
Tetraminion by R.A. Roth

.